THIS WALKER BOOK BELONGS TO:

_____

_____

_____

To my first grandson, Jacob Albert Mann
A. G. H.

To Abbe and Jacob, and to my mom
M. S.

First published 2003 by Walker Books Ltd
87 Vauxhall Walk, London SE11 5HJ

This edition published 2004

2 4 6 8 10 9 7 5 3 1

Text © 2003 Anna Grossnickle Hines
Illustrations © 2003 Melissa Sweet

The right of Anna Grossnickle Hines and Melissa Sweet to be identified as
author and illustrator respectively of this work has been asserted by them
in accordance with the Copyright, Designs and Patents Act 1988

This book has been typeset in Kidprint

Printed in China

British Library Cataloguing in Publication Data:
a catalogue record for this book is available from the British Library

ISBN 1-84428-472-7

www.walkerbooks.co.uk

My Grandma Is Coming to Town

Anna Grossnickle Hines

illustrated by Melissa Sweet

WALKER BOOKS
AND SUBSIDIARIES
LONDON · BOSTON · SYDNEY · AUCKLAND

My grandma lives far away.

When I was a baby, she came to see me.

She taught me a clapping rhyme:

"Pat-a-cake, pat-a-cake, baker's man,
 Bake me a cake as fast as you can;
 Pat it and roll it, and mark it with G,
 Put it in the oven for Grandma and me."

I could only say, "Patta patta, rolla rolla."

Now I can say all the words, but when Grandma calls on the phone, she still says, "Patta patta."
"Rolla rolla," I say.
It is our special way of saying hello. I like to play that telephone game with Grandma.

I have pictures of my Pat-a-Cake Grandma
and she has pictures of me.

She sends me the best surprises ...
like my rhyme book and Nosey.
She said Nosey could give me nose kisses.
Nose kisses make me laugh.

Pat-a-Cake Grandma lives too far away to give me real kisses and hugs so she puts lots of X kisses and O hugs in her letters. I send her X kisses too.

Last week she sent me a letter that said she was coming to see me. I could hardly wait.

Dear Jacob,

Hark, hark, the dogs do bark,
Your Grandma is coming to town.
She'll fly in a great big aeroplane,
Up in the air and down.
Love,
Grandma
XOXOXOXOXOXOXO

I helped Daddy make the bed for Grandma.
Mummy put flowers in her room, and I
made a "Welcome Grandma" sign.

Welcome Grandma

At last the day came. Daddy brought Grandma home from the airport. Mummy gave her a big hug. I just watched.

Daddy said, "Don't you have a hug for your grandma?"
I shook my head. She looked like my Pat-a-Cake
Grandma, only different.

"Patta patta," she said.
She sounded like my Pat-a-Cake Grandma, only closer.

I wanted to say "Rolla rolla", but my mouth couldn't.
I was too shy of this grandma. I played with Nosey
and gave him kisses – nose kisses.

Mummy said, "Do you know who else likes that
kind of kiss?"

I knew it was Grandma, but I only wanted to give
nose kisses to Nosey.

"That's OK," Grandma said. She smiled at me.
I wanted to tell her something so I decided to
call Grandma on my telephone.
"Ring-ring! Ring-ring!"
"I think that must be for me," Grandma said.
"I wonder who it could be. Hello?"

"Patta patta," I said.

"Rolla rolla," said Grandma.

 I said, "It's me, Grandma."

 She said, "I'm so glad to hear your voice."

"I have to go now," I said.

 My Pat-a-Cake Grandma was really here,

 right in our living-room.

Nosey and I fetched the rhyme book.

"Well, look at this," Grandma said. "Maybe I'll read a bit.

Hickety pickety, my black hen,
She lays eggs for gentlemen,
Sometimes nine and sometimes ten."

"Hickety pickety, my black hen," I said, but I only whispered it.

"I know another rhyme," I said.

"Hark, hark, the dogs do bark,
My grandma is coming to town.
She'll fly in a great big aeroplane,
Up in the air and down."

Grandma laughed. "And here I am!" she said.

"I know," I said. "You are my real
 Pat-a-Cake Grandma."
"I certainly am," she said.
"Only something is different," I told her.
"What's that?" she said.
"Now," I said, "instead of O hugs,
 like in our letters, we can have real ones."
"And don't forget the kisses," said Grandma.

She gives me my favourite kind.

WALKER BOOKS is the world's leading
independent publisher of children's books.
Working with the best authors and illustrators
we create books for all ages, from babies
to teenagers – books your child will
grow up with and always remember. So…

FOR THE BEST CHILDREN'S BOOKS,
LOOK FOR THE BEAR